D0111537

This is a work of fiction. Any references to historical events, real people, or real places are used fictitiously. Other names, characters, places, and events are products of the author's imagination, and any resemblance to actual events or places or persons, living or dead, is entirely coincidental.

251 Park Avenue South, New York, NY 10010

Manufactured in China RRD 0520
littlebeebooks.com

Library of Congress Cataloging-in-Publication Data is available upon request.
ISBN 978-1-4998-0764-6 (hc)
First Edition 10 9 8 7 6 5 4 3 2 1
ISBN 978-1-4998-0763-9 (pbk)
First Edition 10 9 8 7 6 5 4 3 2 1

# Tales of SASHA

## The Best Birthday Party Ever

by Alexa Pearl
illustrated by Letizia Rizzo

little bee books

# Contents

CHAPTER 1

# Party Princess

"Don't stop flying!" the silver horse called to Sasha.

He was too late. Sasha began floating on the clouds.

"I want to read this again." Sasha pulled a golden invitation out of an envelope.

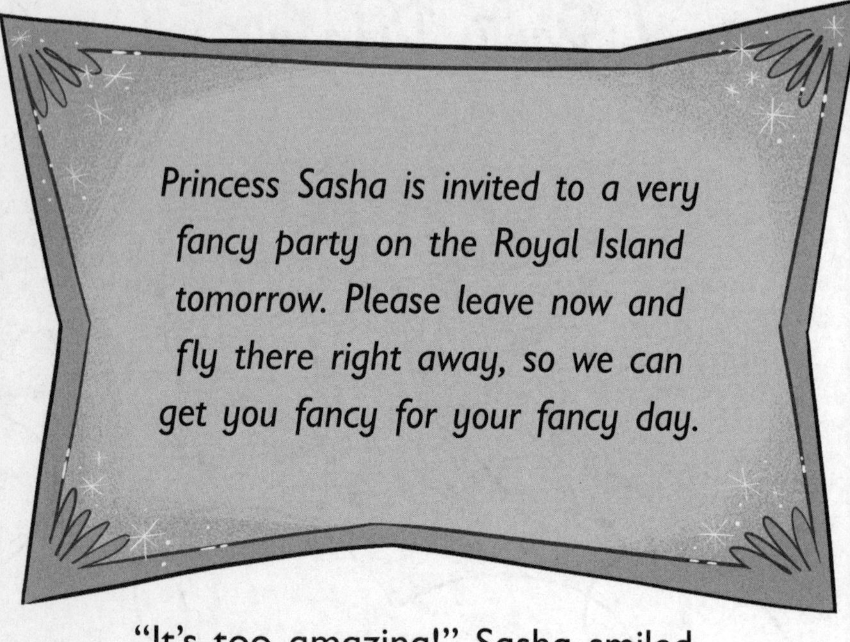


"It's too amazing!" Sasha smiled.

"Which part?" The silver horse glided next to her.

"All of it!" cried Sasha. "First, I found out that I'm a horse that can fly. Then, I found out that I'm also a princess. Now, I'm invited to the Royal Island for a fancy party. And I'm about to get fanci-fied!"

It made Sasha dizzy to say it all out loud.

"It is amazing," said a second silver horse. "Going to a party on the Royal Island is a huge honor."

The two silver horses had been sent by the King and Queen, who rule over all the flying horses around the world. The silver horses were showing Sasha the way to the Royal Island where the King and Queen lived. It was a long flight over the ocean.

"Can you fly fast?" the first silver horse asked Sasha.

"Of course," Sasha said, flying in a loop around the two silver horses.

"Then follow us. Let's go!" The two horses zoomed forward, streaking silver across the blue sky.

Sasha gazed down at the ground. Her friends, Wyatt and Kimani, galloped through the green fields. They looked so tiny from way up here. Sasha waved her tail at them and flew off. She'd see them soon.

Sasha remembered the first time she flew. It wasn't so long ago. She had been galloping through the fields. The little white patch on her gray back suddenly began to itch. Then wings sprouted from that patch! Big, feathered wings that had lifted her into the air.

Flying felt fantastic! She'd had no idea that a horse could fly.

She'd grown up with all four hooves on the ground. But it turned out that she wasn't like the other horses in her valley. Not at all.

The Queen of the flying horses had given birth to Sasha. Then she'd left baby Sasha with a family of non-flying horses. The King and Queen had done this to keep her safe from danger. They wanted to keep their flying princess a secret.

When her wings popped out, she wasn't a secret anymore.

Now, she wore a sparkly crown on her head.

And flying was as easy as galloping.

Now, she was on her way to a princess party on the Royal Island.

Sasha flew fast. She chased a swarm of orange butterflies. She raced a bird with bright blue feathers. She flew up, up, up.

Suddenly, a dark shadow fell over Sasha. Something large was making that shadow. And that something large was flying right above her.

CHAPTER 2

# Come Back!

"Hello, up there!" called Sasha.

An enormous flying leaf soared overhead, and then a horse's nose poked over the side of it. "Hello, down there!"

It was Wyatt! Wyatt was Sasha's better-than-best friend. He rode the magical leaf like a flying surfboard.

Wyatt didn't have wings. He couldn't play cloud tag. He couldn't fly to Crystal Cove, the land of the flying horses. He couldn't soar over the ocean. So, the King and Queen had given Wyatt a flying leaf that would let him fly next to Sasha.

It was the best gift ever.

Sasha tilted up her face. "What are you doing here?"

"You need to—*whoa*!" Wyatt wobbled. His four hooves shot up. He tumbled onto his backside. His rump pushed the leaf down, down, down . . . until it rested on Sasha's head.

Wyatt grinned and scrambled to his feet. "Still working on my balance."

Sasha darted out to fly alongside him.

Wyatt's smile turned into a frown. "I came to tell you that you can't go to the Royal Island."

"Do you miss me already?" teased Sasha. "Is that it?"

"That's not it." Wyatt rolled his eyes and swatted his tail at her. "Do you know what tomorrow is?"

"It's the *best* day of the year," said Sasha. "It's my birthday."

"Exactly! You can't go to the Royal Island on your birthday," said Wyatt.

"Why not?" asked Sasha.

"Because it's your birthday." Wyatt rolled his eyes. "You spend birthdays with your family and your friends and—"

Sasha interrupted him. “I bet the fancy party on the Royal Island is for me. Imagine how amazing a magical, royal birthday party will be. I bet they’ll have frosted-covered fruits, unicorn games, and seahorses singing songs.”

“That sounds nice, but we always celebrate our birthdays together,” Wyatt said quietly. “You and me.”

“Oh.” Sasha now understood why Wyatt had flown after her. He wanted to go to the fancy party with her. “I’m sure I could get an invitation for you, too. You’re my friend, and if it’s a party for me . . .”

“I don’t want to go to *that* party,” cried Wyatt.

"Okay." Sasha was confused. *What did he want?* She looked around. The silver horses were long out of sight. "Wyatt, I really need to get flying."

"No! You can't go. You have to come back to Verdant Valley. I want to celebrate your birthday like we've done every year. You can't just change things," said Wyatt.

"What if I *want* to change things? Just this once?" asked Sasha. "Next year, I will—"

"But the party is tomorrow, not next year!" Wyatt blurted out.

"Party? What party?" asked Sasha.

Wyatt cringed. "Uh-oh. I just blew it."

"What are you talking about?" demanded Sasha.

"Your family is throwing you a big birthday party tomorrow morning. It's supposed to be a surprise." Wyatt grimaced. "Are you . . . surprised?"

Sasha laughed. "Totally surprised!"

CHAPTER 3

# Surprised Face

Sasha had never had a surprise party before. Secretly though, she'd always wanted one.

She'd imagined how it would be. She'd wake up for a morning gallop. Her mother, her father, and her two sisters would jump out from behind the family's cottonwood tree. Wyatt and her school friends would be there, too. They would all yell, "Surprise!" Sasha would rear back, startled. Then she'd nuzzle them all. They'd eat stacks of pancakes with maple syrup.

She would finally have a surprise party this year.

"Your sisters will be angry that I messed up the surprise," said Wyatt.

"No one has to know. I can fake it. Look, here's my surprised face." Sasha opened her eyes extra-wide.

"You look scared," said Wyatt.

Sasha tried again. She opened her mouth and showed all her teeth.

"Now you look mean," said Wyatt.

"I'm trying." Sasha moved her face this way and that way.

"Since you know about the party, you won't go to the Royal Island, right?" asked Wyatt.

*Oh, no!* Sasha had forgotten she was going to the Royal Island for a party. Now there were two birthday parties for her. She wanted to go to both. What should she do?

"You can't miss our party," added Wyatt. "Your family will be so sad if you're not there. I will be, too."

Sasha didn't want to make them sad. "Okay, let me think."

She flew back and forth. She thought and thought.

"I have an idea," she said finally. "I'll fly to the Royal Island now. I'll ask the King and Queen to move their party to the next day. This way, I can go to both parties."

Wyatt let out a *whoop!* "Can you make it back in time? We want to wake you up and surprise you."

"I promise. Cross my hooves or I'll never fly again." Sasha crossed her front hooves. Then she perked up her ears and snorted loudly.

"Are you okay?" asked Wyatt. "What are you doing?"

"It's my new surprised look. Is it good?" asked Sasha

"Well . . . " Wyatt tried to be kind. "I'd lose the snort."

"Really? I liked the snort." Sasha picked up the pace and quickly darted off toward the Royal Island.

"See you soon!" Wyatt waved, then steered his flying leaf back toward Verdant Valley.

Sasha soared across the sky. No birds, butterflies, or horses flew with her. She was all alone now.

All of a sudden, someone yanked her tail!

"*Yeow!*" she cried.

She wasn't alone after all.

CHAPTER 4

# Party #3

Sasha suddenly heard giggling behind her.

"Who's there?" she said, quickly whirling around.

"It's us!" cried Kimani and Collie.

Kimani was a flying horse. Her purple feather wings matched her violet coat, and she always wore braids in her tail. Of the flying horses, Kimani was Sasha's best friend. She lived in Crystal Cove with many other flying horses.

Collie was a plant pixie. She was teeny-tiny and had dandelion-fluff hair and pale green skin. Plant pixies lived inside flowers. They used to be enemies of the flying horses, but not anymore. Plant pixies didn't have wings, so they flew on the backs of hummingbirds. Collie rode Lucia, her special hummingbird.

"What are you guys doing here?" Sasha asked her friends. She'd never had so many in-the-air visitors before.

"Looking for you," said Collie.

"We have a message from the flying horses of Crystal Cove," said Kimani.

"It's from the plant pixies, too," added Collie.

"What is it?" asked Sasha.

"There will be a birthday party in Crystal Cove just for you," said Kimani.

Sasha blinked rapidly. *Another party? That makes three!* she thought in amazement.

"What's wrong?" asked Kimani.

"I'm surprised. Really surprised." Sasha laughed. "But the party on the Royal Island is for my birthday, too."

"It is?" asked Kimani. "Well, at our party, there will be music and dancing on the beach."

"The flamingos, spider monkeys, and rabbits started a band. They've been practicing birthday songs," said Collie. "And every song is about you, Sasha."

"Wow!" Sasha couldn't think of what else to say. She had made so many new friends since she learned she could fly. Now, they all wanted to celebrate her birthday.

"Your face sure looks surprised." Kimani clapped her hooves together.

"Show me the face I just made," begged Sasha.

Kimani sucked in her breath and blinked rapidly.

"I need to make that exact face again tomorrow morning." She told them about Wyatt's surprise party. "Oh, no! When does your party start?"

"At lunchtime," said Kimani.

"That's great! I can go to Verdant Valley in the morning, and then fly to Crystal Cove for lunch," said Sasha. "Everything will work out fine. I just need to get the King and Queen to move their party to the day after tomorrow."

"Do you think they'll do it?" Kimani didn't know the royal family very well.

"I'm sure they will." But Sasha didn't know the royal family much at all, either. She chewed her lip. She didn't want to let down her family or friends.

She had to get to the island as quickly as possible to find out.

CHAPTER 5

# Fanci-fied!

Collie gave Sasha's ear a tiny goodbye kiss. Then she steered Lucia to fly behind Kimani. Kimani headed toward Crystal Cove. She would tell the flying horses that Sasha would be there tomorrow afternoon.

Sasha sniffed the wind and caught the scent of the silver horses. She followed their smell across the wide ocean to an island she had visited once before. The golden shore sparkled brightly in the sun.

Sasha had reached the Royal Island.

She landed on a big rock. Upon seeing her, silver horses nearby cheered and sang out, "Our Lost Princess is here!" They piled flower necklaces around her neck.

Sasha thanked them for the royal greeting. She looked around. The King and Queen were not on the rocky shore.

"May I go to the royal tree house?" she asked the silver horses.

On the Royal Island, the flying horses lived in glittery tree houses.

"No, no, no." The silver horses surrounded her. "They are busy right now. First, you must come with us."

“But, I really need to—” Sasha didn’t get a chance to finish. The silver horses led her across some rocks to a waterfall. Water flowed over a cliff, creating a swirling pool below. Flower petals floated on the warm water. The air smelled of honey and vanilla.

A gold horse with violet eyes greeted them. Her mane and tail were curled into ringlets. Her name was Pashmina, and she looked Sasha up and down.

"Tsk, tsk." She shook her head. "We must get you fancy for the party."

"Okay, but first I want to talk to—" Sasha tried again.

"No time for talking." Pashmina removed the wreaths from Sasha's neck. Then she nudged her into the water. "We have a lot of work to do."

Two muskrats washed her. One massaged lilac shampoo through her mane. The other combed vanilla butter through her tail.

When they were done, a flock of bluebirds held aloft a fluffy towel. Sasha stepped out of the pool. They flew to her and rubbed her dry.

The muskrats braided her tail with hibiscus flowers. They curled her mane. They put her crown on.

Sasha opened her wings. The muskrats then stuck sequins onto her feathers. They sprinkled glitter dust over her entire body.

Sasha looked at herself in the pool's reflecting water. She was so fancy and sparkly. She loved being fanci-fied!

"You're almost ready for our party," said Pashmina.

*Party? Oh, no!* thought Sasha. It had gotten late. The sun was starting to set. "I need to talk to the King and Queen right away."

"Not now. We still have more work to do," said Pashmina.

Sasha thought of Wyatt and her family. She thought of Kimani and Collie. She had promised to be back in time for their parties.

She stood as straight as she could. She made her voice princess-like. "It's super-important. I *must* talk to them immediately."

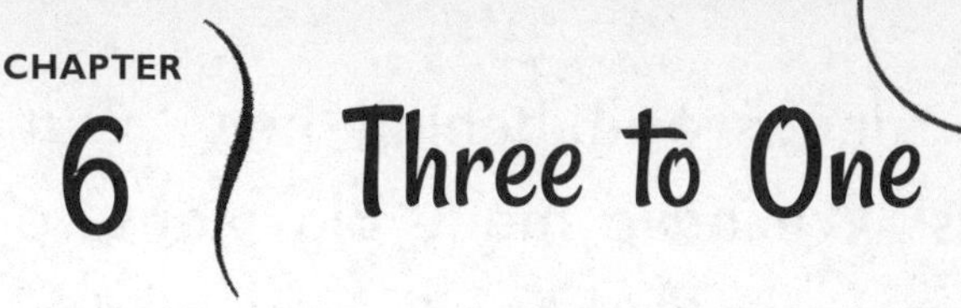

# CHAPTER 6 Three to One

Pashmina listened. She flew Sasha up to the treetops. They landed on the porch of the royal tree house. The front door swung open.

The Queen smiled. “Sasha, we’re so happy to see you! You look beautiful.”

The King stood behind her. "Our princess! We have made big plans to celebrate your birthday. I love parties. Don't you?"

"I do." Sasha followed them inside. "Very much."

"I want this to be your best birthday ever," said the King. "The party will begin first thing tomorrow. First, we'll gather on the island's highest point for a show."

"What kind of show?" asked Sasha.

"As the sun rises, our daredevil horse flying team will do tricks in the sky," said the King. "You can fly with them if you'd like."

"Me? I don't know any tricks."

"They will teach you. After all, it's your birthday! Then you will lead the parade of the royal horses across a rainbow."

"A *real* rainbow?" asked Sasha.

"Yes, a real rainbow. We will feast on sugar oats and eat fruits that no other horses have ever tasted. There will be dancing and magical presents. Some will give you powers far greater than flying."

"That's incredible!" Sasha bounced up and down on her hooves. She wanted to walk on a rainbow. She wanted to open her magical presents. She couldn't wait!

"Your party starts bright and early tomorrow morning," said the Queen. "We have a tree house for you to sleep in tonight, so you can get a good rest."

Sasha hesitated. The royal party sounded *so* good. But she'd promised to go to Wyatt and Kimani's parties tomorrow.

"Is there any way to, uh . . . make my party a different day?" asked Sasha.

"A different day? Your birthday is tomorrow. That is the day we should celebrate." The Queen looked confused.

Sasha told them about the other parties.

"The daredevil team will only be on the island tomorrow. They leave at midnight for shows on the other side of the world," said the King. "They will be back next month. Maybe we can move your party to then?"

Sasha didn't know what to do. There were three parties and only one of her. And she didn't want to wait so long for the royal party.

"Can I invite Wyatt, Kimani, and Collie to the party?" she asked the King and Queen.

"I know they're your best friends, but only royal horses may go to a party on the Royal Island. It's a rule that cannot be broken. Not even by me." The King sighed.

Sasha hung her head. A tear trickled down her cheek. She loved both of her families. She loved all of her friends. She would end up disappointing someone.

*My birthday is going to be horrible*, she thought.

"Don't cry." The King wiped away her tear. "You can't be sad on your birthday."

"I agree. Only birthday smiles. I have a plan, but it won't be easy, Sasha," said the Queen. "We will move the royal party to tomorrow evening. It will be a sunset party instead of a sunrise party. You can go to the breakfast surprise party in Verdant Valley. Then you can go to the lunch party in Crystal Cove. After that, you can fly back here for a dinner party. Can you do all that?"

"No problem!" Sasha perked up. She nuzzled them. "Thank you! I better start flying back and tell everyone."

The Queen looked out the door. Night had fallen. The crescent moon didn't light the dark sky.

"You won't be able to find your way," said the Queen. "Sleep here. The royal guards will wake you just before the sun rises. I will make sure of it. In fact, I will wake you myself. Then I can be the first to wish you a happy birthday."

Sasha looked at the night sky. It was a long trip back, and she was very tired after flying all this way. "Thank you," she said. "That's a good idea."

She was taken to a beautiful tree house with a thick straw mat on the floor.

Pashmina came in. She wrapped special netting around Sasha so her fanci-fied mane and tail wouldn't get messed up. Then the King and Queen kissed her good night.

Sasha closed her eyes. She was eager to sleep. The faster she went to sleep, the faster her birthday and her three parties would come.

She waited.

And waited.

And waited.

She could not fall asleep.

CHAPTER 7

# Going Home

Sasha heard an owl hoot. Then silence. She stared at the ceiling.

*Why can't I sleep?* she wondered. *Am I too excited?*

Sasha was excited, but that wasn't keeping her awake.

The tree house felt wrong.

The straw mat felt wrong.

Waking up on her birthday on the Royal Island felt wrong.

She wanted to sleep next to her sisters under their cottonwood tree in Verdant Valley. She wanted to wake up to the birds singing her a birthday song. She wanted to eat her mother's pancakes for breakfast.

That's how her birthday had always been. And that's how she wanted it to stay.

*I have to go back NOW*, she realized. *I have to get home before they wake up.*

Sasha bolted upright, then froze. The netting around her curly mane tangled around her. She was trapped!

She bucked and arched her neck. Finally, it fell away.

Sasha hurried out to the porch. All the royal horses were asleep. She spotted a snow-white owl on a nearby branch.

The owl began to hoot and hoot.

Sasha's heart beat fast. The royal horses would wake up. They would want to know what she was doing. She had to keep the owl quiet.

"Pease, don't hoot!" She spotted a basket of fruits Pashmina had left her. "Are you hungry?" she asked the owl. "Do you want to share a midnight snack?"

The owl stopped hooting. She flew to the porch. She poked her beak into the basket. "Can I pick first?"

"You can have all of it," said Sasha. "As long as you stay quiet."

The owl ate a strawberry. "I've never met a flying horse who was awake at night like I am."

"I'm not usually up this late. I need to fly back home." Sasha searched the sky. "How do you find your way in the dark?"

"Don't you have night vision like me?" asked the owl.

"I don't," said Sasha.

“Too bad. Then use the stars. They will guide you,” said the owl.

Sasha looked up. There were hundreds of stars. “Can you show me how?”

With her wing, the owl pointed—star by star—the way she should go. From the big star to the little star to the bright star. Sasha tried to memorize the way.

“Tell the King and Queen I will be back tomorrow night for the party,” she told the owl.

The owl nodded. She had a plum in her beak.

Sasha began to follow the stars. She hoped they would lead her home.

CHAPTER 8

# Shooting Star

Sasha flew from star to star, using them as a map.

The night air was cool. She spotted the bright star. She flew toward it.

The star moved. Sasha followed it. The star kept moving. Sasha chased it. It zoomed across the sky.

*How strange!* thought Sasha. No other star in the sky had moved. And then she understood.

This star was a shooting star.

Oh, no! Sasha had followed it. Now she wasn't where the owl had told her to go. Looking around, she didn't recognize any stars in the sky. The fields below were dark. She didn't recognize them, either.

Sasha spun around and around. Which direction should she fly in next?

She had no idea. She was totally lost.

She stopped flapping her wings. Suddenly, she began to fall from the sky. Down, down, down . . .

Quickly, she picked a direction. She flapped her wings and flew. *I hope this leads home*, thought Sasha.

Sasha flew for hours. The sun began to rise. It was officially her birthday. Sasha looked down, hoping to see Verdant Valley.

All she saw was water. Sasha was flying over the ocean, and Verdant Valley wasn't near the ocean. Her stomach dropped.

She wasn't in Verdant Valley being woken up by her family.

She wasn't on the Royal Island being woken up by the Queen.

She was in the sky, all alone.

Sasha spotted a huge sandbar in the ocean. Her wings were tired. Her eyes were heavy with sleep. She decided to land there.

The wet sand crunched under her hooves when she touched down. There was only one palm tree in sight, and she lay underneath it. Sasha watched the waves wash up onto the beach. The sun slowly began to brighten the sky.

*I was supposed to have three parties today,* she thought. *I was supposed to celebrate with every horse and magical creature that I love. Now, I'm by myself.*

Sasha used her front hoof to write *Happy Birthday Sasha* in the sand.

She built a sand cake. She stuck a palm frond on top of the cake and pretended it was a candle. With a big *whoosh*, Sasha blew out her pretend candle.

Sand flew everywhere!

Sasha shook the sand from her body. She no longer looked fancy. Her mane and tail were full of knots and sand.

She was too tired to care.

She closed her eyes and fell into a deep, deep sleep.

# CHAPTER 9 Seagull Search Party

Something sharp jabbed Sasha's back. Her eyes fluttered open.

She felt the jab again. Pinpricks danced along her back.

"Ouch!" Sasha was fully awake now. Three seagulls stood on her back. Their claws dug into her. "Get off of me!"

The birds took to the air. They joined a huge flock circling overhead. Then the three seagulls came back down and landed on the hot sand beside Sasha.

"Good afternoon," a large seagull with silver feathers greeted her.

"Afternoon?" Sasha squinted, looking up. The sun was high in the sky. She'd been asleep for a long time. "Is it still my birthday?"

"It is," said the silver seagull. "That is why we came to find you."

"Find me?" Sasha was confused. "Who are you?"

"I am the search seagull from the Royal Island. The Queen called me. My flock has been looking for you all day." He pointed to a group of silver and gold-feathered birds above.

The second seagull stepped forward. He had rainbow-colored feathers. "I am the search seagull from Crystal Cove. You didn't come for your lunchtime party. My flock was also sent to find you." Each bird in his flock had a different color of the rainbow feathers.

The third seagull stepped forward. She had regular gray feathers. “I am the search seagull from Verdant Valley. You weren’t there for your morning surprise. Your family and friends sent me to find you.”

Sasha grinned. Everyone had sent out a search seagull for her. “How did you find me?”

"We spotted your birthday message in the sand," said the gray seagull.

"The day is almost over," said the silver seagull. "There is only time for us to take you to one party."

"Which one will it be?" asked the rainbow seagull.

# CHAPTER 10 Party Time!

Sasha made up her mind. "I'm going home to Verdant Valley."

She paused, thinking. "I need you to bring a special message to Kimani, Collie, and the flying horses of Crystal Cove." She whispered into the rainbow seagull's ear.

"And I'll need you to bring a special message to the King and Queen on the Royal Island." She whispered into the silver seagull's ear.

Both birds flew off. Sasha followed the gray seagull to Verdant Valley. She was glad he knew the way home.

Soon, Sasha spotted her family's cottonwood tree. It was decorated with birthday garlands. She saw her mother, her father, her sisters, and Wyatt standing under it.

"Watch this," she told the seagull. Sasha put on a burst of speed and zoomed down. As her hooves touched the grass, she cried, "Surprise!"

Her mother and father were startled. Her sisters let out loud whinnies. Wyatt reared back and made the best surprised face ever.

"It's a surprise party!" cried Sasha.

Everyone was so happy to see Sasha. Her mom quickly gathered the birds in the tree and had them sing a birthday song. Then she pulled out a platter of pancakes.

"I'm sorry your birthday pancakes are cold," she told Sasha. "I made them early this morning."

"I like them cold." Sasha took a big bite. Then another. "Could you please make more?"

"More pancakes? Sure!" said her mom. "How many?"

"Fifty pancakes," said Sasha.

"Fifty?!" Her mom tilted her head. "Why are you so hungry?"

"The pancakes aren't for me. They're for my guests. I'm throwing myself my own birthday party," announced Sasha. "And you're all invited."

"Who else is coming?" asked Wyatt.

At that moment, a rainbow appeared in the sky. But it wasn't a real rainbow. It was the brightly colored flying horses from Crystal Cove. Kimani had led them to Sasha's party. The horses carried flowers, streamers, and balloons from the party they'd planned in Crystal Cove.

“Happy birthday!” Collie said, peeling back the petals of a flower to reveal herself. She poked out her head. Plant pixies suddenly popped out of all the flowers.

Loud music floated in from the mountains. A group of flamingos, spider monkeys, and rabbits playing instruments came into view. They were the party band from Crystal Cove.

"You brought all three parties together?" asked Wyatt.

"I tried to, but the King and Queen aren't here." Sasha worried they wouldn't leave the Royal Island for a party without magic. She watched the sky. For the longest time, it stayed empty.

Then she saw streaks of silver. Gold sparkles began raining down. The King and Queen had arrived!

"Happy birthday to our princess." They landed and hugged Sasha.

"I'm such a mess," apologized Sasha. "And this party isn't fancy."

"We don't need fancy," said the Queen. "We only want you to be happy on your birthday."

"I *am* happy." Sasha looked around. "Having everyone I love here together makes me the happiest of all!"

Sasha introduced the King and Queen to her parents and sisters. Kimani and Wyatt gathered around. They all celebrated Sasha.

"And I have a surprise for you. Look up," said the Queen.

The daredevil flying horse team shot through the sky, doing tricks. Sasha joined them. This was definitely the best birthday party ever.

**Journey to some magical places and outer space, rock out, and find your inner superhero with these other chapter book series from Little Bee Books!**

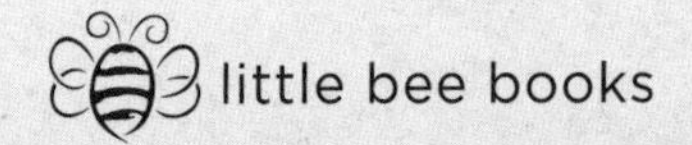

Read on for a sneak peek of the **ISLE OF MISFITS** series.

chapter one

# THE LONELIEST GARGOYLE

Gibbon the gargoyle lived atop the same castle all his life. Gargoyles were meant to protect the buildings they lived on. Sometimes, that meant protecting the people inside those buildings, too. That's what Gibbon was always taught.

But Gibbon couldn't stay still in one place *all* day. Sure, it was what he was *supposed* to do, but it was so boring! So Gibbon found something new to do to pass the time: playing pranks on people as they walked by below.

And winter was his favorite season for pranks. Winter meant snowballs.

One snowy day, he saw a man in a suit hurrying by the castle. Gibbon quickly made a snowball in his hands. He held it over the edge and dropped it, watching as it hit the man right on the head.

The man jumped from the shock of the cold snow. A confused look crossed his face when he didn't see anyone around.

Holding back laughter, Gibbon rolled another snowball and dropped it on the man. This time, the man yelped and ran off.

"*Gibbon!*" a voice whispered harshly.

He jumped and turned toward the gargoyle speaking to him. Elroy was the leader of the castle gargoyles and almost never broke his silence.

"That's enough," Elroy ordered. "You are too old to be playing pranks on the humans. You need to start taking your post seriously."

"But it's so boring!" Gibbon protested. "We just stand around all day. Even at night, we do nothing! Who are we even defending the castle from anyway?"

Elroy did not move, but his eyes glared over at Gibbon. "You need to learn how to work with your team, Gibbon. Your slacking off only makes it harder for the rest of us."

With a sigh, Gibbon looked down at the street. He watched as a group of kids stopped below the castle. One of them picked up some snow and threw it at another. Instead of getting mad, the other kid started laughing and made his own snowball. In no time at all, the kids were in a full-fledged snowball fight!

*Maybe if I can get Elroy to play, everyone else will loosen up!* he thought.

Gibbon smiled at Elroy. "Hey, catch me if you can! If you do, I'll be quiet and guard the castle the rest of the day!"

With a laugh, Gibbon took off. He climbed down the side of the castle, then darted down an empty street.

Gibbon knew—he just *knew*—if Elroy played with him, he'd understand.

But when he stopped and looked back, he didn't see Elroy. His heart sank.